TALES FROM AIREGIN VILLAGE

(A SATIRE)

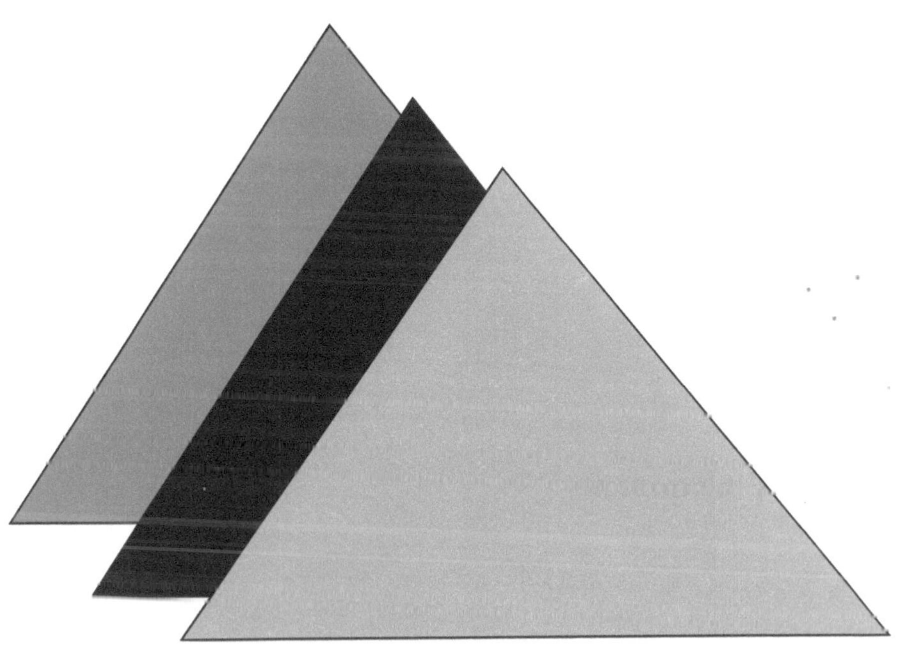

Exradallenum Olusegun Akinsanya, 2020

email: *exradallenum140122001@gmail.com*,
whatsApp: +2348063345539, 07064382018

Cover Art Picture from Contemporary-African-Art.com and face2faceafrica.com

Designed by The Harbinger Concept (Nigeria)

ISBN: 978-978-983-748-9

Readers' Comments

Within the spate of one hour, I was literally glued and finished your Satire, **Tales from Airegin Village**. I must confess that the book is indeed an extraordinary repertoire; very instructive, meaningful and eye opening. I cannot agree less that wealth, power and affluence are the true tests of virtues, character and identity. I must salute you for that beautiful piece Sir. The satire brings to my recollection the concluding verses in William Shakespeare's book titled Measure to Measure wherein it was stated that 'Man proud Man, dressed in a little brief authority. Plays such fantastic tricks against high heavens that even the angels weep'.
Ayotunde O. Okunowo, Ijebu-Imusin, Ogun State, Nigeria

Saint Segun, the dreamer, I read the book this afternoon; very brilliant piece of work. The great Wole Soyinka himself would be proud of the work. God bless you and increase your knowledge. Well done my friend.

also enjoyed the final story of a man torn between loves and the decisions he made. The last story was an interesting way to illustrate the distinction from our idealism as youth and then what happens when we are put in situations where power becomes possible. It seems to be one of the tragedies of the Nigerian political situation, from the little I know about Nigerian politics. ***Jo de Silva, Policy and Communications expert, Fullurton, SA***

ACKNOWLEDGEMENT

I sincerely thank the people who made sterling contributions to my growth into being the character that I have grown to become. I also wish to thank the women who were part of my love life while growing up. I thank my friends who share my views on the need for Africa to have a rebirth. The names of the characters I have used in this book are the names of some of the special people that had lasting impacts on my life.

DEDICATION

Just like the claps of transient thunders

And glitters of fleeting lightenings

In the day that rain threatened but failed

Gani dissolved into a fairy tale

Gani Fawehinmi (1938 – 2009)

Gani fought against social injustice in a country known

for corruption, nepotism and oppression of the poor

BOOK ONE

CHAPTER ONE

I WAS SHORTLISTED FOR A WRITING COMPETITION

It was my turn to read the article I submitted for an international writing competition, before a panel of judges and my fellow contestants. The prize money was $10,000. The process was too rigorous...

My friend Tunji, a Mass Communication graduate from Lagos State University introduced the competition to me and persuaded me to send in an article for the competition. Tunji graduated with a Second Class Upper while I graduated with a First Class degree. He was very good at writing long essays and short stories. He had freelanced for a number of blogs and online magazines. I didn't do communications, I did Education. I found myself inferior to him when it comes to creative writing.

When he told me about the writing competition, I was so excited. Actually, it was the price tag that caught my attention - nothing more! Immediately he handed the printed flier of the competition to me, I did a mental calculation of the Naira equivalence of $10,000. That was something in the neighbourhood of 3.5 million Naira. I deducted 1 million Naira, which was the price of a plot of land I would buy at a remote village at Ibeju Lekki. I would be left with 2.5 million Naira. Then, I calculated the amount of blocks I needed to build a ten-room school complex. I knew the money wouldn't be enough, but at least I would get the work to a point before I sought for help from well-wishers and relatives.

Wow, I was daydreaming! I'd not even applied, but I had spent the prize money in my head. I heard that over 5,000 young writers had applied from all over Africa. The sponsor of the award was a young African, who was a professor of Anthropology in an American university. He really loved creative writing. He posted articles on Facebook every week.

After going through over 100 articles that I had written and sent to my friends on WhatsApp, I decided to submit the article I titled "The Village Mindset." The condition given by the board that oversees the award was that any article to be submitted should be the original thought of the writer and should not have been published for commercial purposes at any time.

A month after I submitted the article, I received an email that I had been selected to participate in a short time creative writing training in a university at Accra, Ghana. I was among the 5 shortlisted candidates from Nigeria. Unfortunately, Tunji was not shortlisted. I informed him that I had been selected. He, a good jolly fellow, wished me well and bade me a safe journey.

CHAPTER TWO

MY EXPERIENCE AT THE WRITING COMPETITION IN GHANA

The organisers of the award paid for my flight to and from Ghana. That was my first time in Ghana at that time. It was such a wonderful experience in the air. Up till that moment, I never really knew I could make a career from writing short stories. I had previously written for fun and sent my stuff to friends who sometimes complained that I bothered them with too many write-ups.

We were taken to a hotel room where we spent the night. In the morning, we were driven in a luxurious bus to the main campus of the University of Ghana for a mentorship programme. For the next two days, a professor in the Department of English trained us on the techniques of creative writing. He emphasised that we shouldn't bother about correcting mistakes while writing the first draft. He said the words should flow from the heart through our fingers to the laptop.

On the third day, we were asked to take turns to read the articles we had submitted for the competition. We were 50 contestants in total, from 10 different countries in Africa. I was assigned number 47. As I sat down on the left side of the multipurpose hall, on the fifth roll, I listened to well scripted articles that were read with beauty and finesse by tongues that had been polished for years in language laboratories. To be honest, I was confused at a point. But I consoled myself that at least I had achieved an extraordinary feat by being shortlisted. It would be best if I went out before my number was called. May be if I didn't make any appearance, they would move on to the next contestant. I lost confidence in my capability to deliver on a big stage, since it was my first time. But when I looked behind me, the door was already shut and some delicately looking ushers were stationed at all the exit points. I was stuck.

I never knew I was lost in thought until someone gently placed a soft palm on my shoulder and informed me that it was my turn. I started coughing profusely. I never had cough before I got to the hall. Few people around me sympathised with me. One of the ushers gave me bottled water. I took a sip, picked my printed article and made for the podium.

...As I stood before an agitated audience and very critical academics that constituted the panel, I wished the electric supply would cut off so that no one would hear what I had to read. I didn't know that I had taken a minute without uttering a word. One of the members of the panel, Professor Appia, said, "young man, you had spent a minute without saying a word! Is it part of the dramatic build up for a great presentation?" I knew he wanted to help me, so I decided to accept that timely help.

Before I started reading my article, I paid a glowing tribute to the Professor that sponsored the competition. I greeted the members of the panel; afterwards I saluted the gallant soldiers that were trying to win the price money instead of me. I really didn't know how to speak Queen's English, so I used my native Yoruba tongue to read the article I submitted for the competition.

CHAPTER THREE

I PRESENTED MY ARTICLE TITLED THE VILLAGE MINDSET AT THE PITCH

THE VILLAGE MINDSET

Few things caught my fancy as a young boy: air flight across continents, a university first class degree, a beautiful baby girl as my daughter, good pulpit skill as a preacher, good writing skill as a writer and an original ideology as a thinker. Each time I read about anyone who's got any of those, something would tingle inside my heart. I felt life was worthless without any of those. I loved to just have those extraordinary experiences.

After achieving these petty stuffs that I set as my primary objectives in life, I discovered that I had fundamental flaws in my goal setting and overall understanding of the realities of life. For each of my achievements I saw someone with something far better. I saw a man on TV with tens of PhD's and who had won a Nobel Laureate twice...

Growing up in a village makes one have peace of mind and value humanity and nature; but it limits one's worldview. It makes one feel good about petty achievements. That's always the limiting factor in not seeing beyond the village and mentality of the people in there.

Village in this context may not be geographical. It's sometimes psychological. Sometimes, the leadership of the people can condition them to have the village mentality. Take for instance, the leaders may build a road using the money contributed by the people (as tax); yet the people would praise them for being God sent as if they did them a favour. The leaders are praised for paying 2 out of 10 months' salaries due to the work force. Some people are conditioned by religious leaders to have the village mentality. They believe everything said; and are even compelled to do the most disgusting things in the name of religion...

I heard of a young businessman who on his first journey to Dubai, got so carried away by the beauty of the airport, started raining curses on Nigerian leaders; past and present. That was the first time he had a glimpse of the life outside the village and got a partial deliverance from the village mentality.

There is a world beyond the current one you are bragging about. There is more to life than what you think you already have. The (leaders) gatekeepers have limited the vision and imagination of the people. They use the instrumentality of politics and religion to restrict the vision of the people. The masses, compelled by myopic vision, then set shallow goals. They paint the picture of a faraway Paradise which can only be attained when one endures hardships and inhuman treatments in this village. They describe genuine urge for excellence and success as covetousness. They encourage people to be realistic and endure (current) hardships. Yet, they and their children go far away from the village to taste the semblance of the Paradise they claimed was an afterlife experience. They designed the school curriculum so as to restrict the thinking of the people to the village mindset, while their children go to Paradise to learn how to really be alive. They teach us in religious centres to defend our faith by strapping bombs on our chest while their children are far away in the Paradise learning to enjoy their Paradise here and now.

When will we be free from yesterday? In our elementary schools we still study A for Apple; in our colleges we still study Abacus is counting device; in our Universities we still memorise Dalton's atomic laws! On Fridays, they teach us to be violent, on Sundays, they teach us to be gullible, docile and gentle. They show us how patriotic it is to live and develop the village, while they and their children only holiday in the village, but enjoy their wealth in the Paradise...

I actually grew up in the village, I have visited a few towns; the village life is better since I am an indigent (son of the soil) which gives me some rights. The only right I don't have is the right to be the head of the village since the list of the leaders to rule for the next hundred years had been written before I was born.

Immediately I finished reading my article, I took a bow and left for my seat. I noticed that Professor Abadoo kept on shaking his head sideways as I made for my seat. Whatever that meant I didn't know, since I didn't understand what that gesture meant in Ghana. If it were to be among the Yoruba tribe in Southwest of Nigeria, I would have understood that it implied a woeful performance.

The other remaining contestants *read their articles,* and we all went for dinner break. Immediately after the dinner, we came back to the hall for the grand finale where the best three articles would be announced and the next instruction would be given. As we filed into the hall, I took pictures with some contestants from Ghana, Cameroon, Togo and South Africa. We also exchanged WhatsApp and email contacts.

CHAPTER FOUR

I WAS SELECTED FOR THE LAST ROUND

By the time we got back to the hall, it had worn a new look. We were thoroughly entertained by the University drama and choral troupes. We were all asked to say one or two things that we learnt during the mentorship session. It was really a time for fun; and it was deliberate. They knew we were all set on edge.

The leader of the team, Professor Abadoo, thanked the university management for making the university hall available for the programme. He appreciated the Local Organising Committee. He also thanked every member of the panel. Then, he asked Ms. Sanders, an associate professor from a university in Texas, to announce the three lucky winners.

I thought within myself that I wouldn't be part of the three. So, I took my phone and started uploading the pictures I took on my Facebook page. The only thing on my mind was my journey back to Lagos.

"Stand up, 47!" I heard a sweet sonorous voice repeat that twice. Honestly, I had forgotten that I was 47! I jumped up to a great applause from everyone. I didn't hear what the instruction was. I was so busy with the social media. Then my neighbour quietly whispered that we were to go to the podium. I moved very quickly to join a lady from South Africa and a young guy from Tanzania. I thought we would be handed a cheque of $10,000 each or maybe a fraction of that based on our position, but I was wrong.

We were given a laptop each and told to write a defence of the main idea behind the article. They gave us one week to write an elaborate work that would reflect the main idea behind the theme of the article, draw some conclusions and make valuable recommendations.

I shook hands with the panellists, embraced some of my colleagues and went inside the bus. All along, I kept on wondering what I should write. I knew that the main idea behind my article was the exploitation of the poor Africans by the religious, political and economic oligarchies.

When I got to my hotel room, I took a shower, put on my pyjamas, and slept off. Then, I had a dream:

CHAPTER FIVE

I HAD A DREAM

In my dream, I met myself on top of a Baobab tree, sitting comfortably like a baboon. I was a passive observer of the social interactions in an animal kingdom.

The name of the kingdom was Airegin village. It was such a wonderful village with good agrarian soil. It had a beehive on the southern part. There were a lot honey bees in the southern part. I only saw drooping honey. How it came about, I couldn't tell because it was so distant from me. I also saw a lot of dusts in the southern part, each time it rained; the dusts caked and formed strong crystals. I saw some shinning metal-like objects and something that looked like charcoal from a long distance (I don't think it was charcoal, but it was dark and precious). I saw that *dew* wet the soil from time to time. Everything painted a picture of wealth and glamour.

I looked towards the North and I saw beautiful trees and many *kwashiorkored* animals. There were metals of different shapes and colours. I saw a lot of movements from one end of the North to the other. I also saw some animals crossing from North to South. But most of the animals that migrated from one part of the

North to South seemed to have a particular strip of land they made their destination of choice. In that place of choice, I saw tall anthills, holes, nests and other signs of habitation.. I also saw a lot of seeds being moved from place to place.

Between the North and the South was a small forest. It had tall trees and shrubs. It was well *grassed* and had a lot of big holes and dunghills. In that small forest called Ajuba, resided animals that controlled the kingdom.

At the central part of Ajuba were the sleekly Snake, the scorching Scorpion, the sly Squirrel, the tantalising Tortoise and spurious Snail. Whatever they decided at the forest of Ajuba dictated what happened in the whole of the village.

Outside of the village was a big town which was far away. For any animal to get to that big town (which was named Mini-Paradise) he had to cross a mighty ocean. There were cruel and hostile alligators, crocodiles and sharks in the ocean. The custodians of the far away town also had dangerous hippopotamuses at the river bank. A lot of animals who had attempted to cross, in order to feel the breeze of Mini-Paradise, had ended up as meals for the hippos and their carcasses used to build the barricades at the bank of the ocean. It was not all the animals that attempted the dangerous journey who died in the process. Some made it. Those who made it were compelled to pack the *dungs* of the higher animals in the town. They could be lucky to help carry the higher animals about town as their *chauffeur*. Sometimes they were used as sacrifices during the fights against hostile towns. Many wished they could come back to Airegin village, but the shame of home return without any material possessions and the harsh conditions of the village deterred them.

My attention was drawn back to the forest where there was an interesting activity in the forest. The meeting was called the Destiny Decider Meeting (DDM). In attendance were the privileged animals that regulated the destinies of the villagers. The prominent among them were Snake and Scorpion. They were the law so they were above the law. Whoever they decided should die, would die. In the day Snake and Scorpion were sworn enemies, but in the night, they shared the spoils. In attendance were also Snail and Tortoise. Both of them had big shells which they used to store the wealth of the people. They appeared slow and harmless; but they ruled the minds of other animals. They were called the *gods*. Both of them had different shells, but the purpose of their shells was the same; that is, to siphon the common wealth of the village as they moved sluggishly across the North and the South of the village. They also had friends in the ocean and allies in the town that helped them transport the wealth inside their shells to the choice places of the far away town. Squirrel was also present. He was very cunning. He understood the content of the soil and the days the rain would fall. He understood what to do with the metals which were scattered in different parts of the village. He manipulated the mood of the village. If he was happy, the village would be happy. If he was sad, the nation would be sad. The law and the *gods* obeyed his instructions.

In my dream, I saw that all these *privileged* animals started discussing. It was a long meeting. It was held inside a deep hole. It was held in thick darkness. It was held while all other animals were fast asleep. The first thing I saw was that each of the privileged animals came in for the meeting in a bizarre manner. They all walked in with their heads down and their tails up. That caught my attention. I couldn't see them very clearly. I wished the place where they were having the meeting was a bit brighter. As I thought about it, I saw a glimpse of light beam to the centre of their meeting place. Then I saw a special meal in a small cocoon. As they filed in, they reverted to their natural standing positions, used their mouth to pick a morsel of the meal, chewed it in silence, drank from a small bowl and then leaned against the wall. I saw a large smoke arise from the corner and they were all subsumed in its thick cover. I saw nothing again for what seemed to be about 5 minutes. By the time the smoke cleared off, I saw all the animals on top of each other. Then I saw nothing again for another few minutes. It was so dark. By the time the brightness appeared, I met myself at the entrance of the hole.

Since I did not witness the beginning of the meeting, I missed the opportunity to observe the rituals that preceded the meeting. Snake was the one that presided over the meeting. He welcomed everyone to the meeting and asked them to give the account of their stewardship for the previous week. That was when it dawned on me that the meeting was on a weekly basis.

Scorpion was the first to talk. "The *manipulators* of the kingdom, I salute you. The events of the past 7 days in our kingdom have shown me that our people are still not aware that Snake and I are one of a kind. On Monday, 15 members of Snake Progressive Party were killed by members of my party, Scorpion Democratic Party. I deliberately asked them to kill those idiots so that there would be violence in that part of the kingdom. Everyone that heard, condemned Snake as being incompetent, but it was part of the game plan. I made myself popular, by sympathising with the family of the deceased while Snake Progressive Party became richer by putting more funds in security department and setting up a commission to care for the children of the deceased." Immediately he sat down, all the animals nodded in appreciation. Snake commented that it was a win-win situation for the political class and the foreign crocodiles that were paid to carry out the attack. He concluded by saying that it only cost the kingdom 100 gallons (about 76 litres) of honey to pay off the foreign crocodiles.

The next animal to speak was Tortoise. He greeted everyone in a language I could not understand. But all of them answered in that same language. As he rose to speak, I saw his golden shell. It shone like a strip aluminium metal under the hot sun. Then he began to speak, "Our people are gullible! I came back from the town two days ago. I went to acquire this new golden shell. The animals that believe in my ideology gave me a lot of treasures. I stuck them under my shell. Immediately I got to the town, I acquired a new shell and bought a new mansion which will serve as my retirement home. I also got new information from higher animals on how to manipulate the animals in the village. I told them they must fight to secure their passage to a higher town beyond the sky. I planted fear and hate in their heart. They must have hate in their hearts in order to be willing and useful tools in my hands. By the time I came back, I only gave one lecture, just one lecture! Then blood started flowing from North to South. I didn't use any *magic*, it was just simple logic!" Then he took his seat.

It was Snail's turn to talk. But he was interrupted by Squirrel. Squirrel jumped to his feet and shouted: "caution, caution,

caution!" Then he continued, "My privileged colleagues, we agreed that only 25 animals should die per week. But last week alone, 40 animals died. Do you realise that the leader of the town told us in the meeting we had with him 2 weeks' ago that we needed to grow the population of the animal village in order to favour the business interest of the town?! Caution, caution, caution!" he warned.

Then Snake beckoned on Snail to talk. "My privileged colleague," Snail started in his usual sluggish and sloppy manner, "my approach this week has never changed from my previous approach. Before the people, I act slowly. I persuade them to be calm and gentle in the face of oppression and opposition. My strategy is very effective. I encourage them to see through my eyes, hear through my cars and think through my brains. I tell them when to sleep and when to wake. I dominate their thoughts. While they aspire to be like me (and adopt my sluggish disposition), I become dangerously rich. I change my shell every week and live like the king of the upper town kingdom. I didn't fill their hearts with hate; rather I filled it with self love and desire to possess a larger portion of the animal kingdom. The more properties they possess, the larger my own share of the spoil!"

Squirrel took his turn to talk. He informed them about what he had done to reduce the population of very wise animals by encouraging them to go the town to become slaves to higher animals. He also told the privileged animals that he had encouraged Snake to add to the daily wages of work animals, but return the increase through shrewd means of increased levies and higher service charges. He said that he had worked very hard to make the currency lose its worth based on the recommendation of higher animals. He concluded by saying that the poorer and less relevantly educated the people were, the easier it would be for them to be governed, controlled and kept in check.

After listening to the privileged class, Snake informed Scorpion to form another party and make Monkey the leader. He asked Squirrel to calculate the amount of banana that would be needed to make the Monkey Alliance Party well-fed. He said the Monkey Alliance Party was to be used as a distraction for the next election. Scorpion quickly reminded Snake of the time he, that is, Scorpion, would take over as the next leader. Snake told him that he was aware. He said that was why he asked Scorpion to set up the Monkey Alliance Party as a form of distraction. The real power belongs to the Snake Progressive Party and Scorpion Democratic Party. He eulogised the efforts of Tortoise and Snail and asked them to come for their share of allocation of animal kingdom resources. But he cautioned Tortoise to be careful not to grant interviews to journalist Parrot. This would prevent Parrot from linking the incessant killings instigated by Tortoise to religion. He also cautioned Snail that his sluggish approach should be altered a little so as to draw a little attention away from Tortoise.

The meeting lasted about 30 minutes. Then Snake gave each one of them a venomous bite which made them hysterical.

CHAPTER SIX

I SHOULD HAVE TAKEN MY DREAM SERIOUSLY

"Segun, you're snoring too loudly!" That was followed by a gentle trudge from Andrews, my South African bed mate. I woke up and looked at him as if he were Snake in the dream I just had. He expressed concern over the way I looked at him. I said nothing to him. I just stood up and went to the convenience.

My journey back to Nigeria was not as exciting as the anticipation that heralded my initial journey. I landed at Murtala Mohammed airport at about 2.08pm the afternoon that succeeded the midnight I had the dream. As instructed, I sent my analysis and the rationale behind my article to the organisers of the award ceremony. I wrote a lengthy academic paper, which more or less was a review of textbooks, Newspaper articles, journals and blogs write-ups on the problems of politics, religion and mismanagement of economy in Nigeria. I quoted extensively from the works of Karl Max, Max Webber, etc. I also quoted copiously from Walter Rodney's book "How Europe underdeveloped Africa."

To be honest, I thought I did a great job with the review. But the email I got was that, though my initial article was adjudged the best, my review did not portend originality. The $10,000 was given to the South African lady who was on the podium with me. I read her work. It was superb. She linked recession in South Africa to the xenophobic attacks on foreigners that own up to 40% of the Small and Medium enterprises in her country. She then linked it with the economic downturn that the Egyptians suffered when the Israelites left their country. It was such a great work. I came second, so I was given a one week all-expenses paid trip to United Arab Emirates.

Before I travelled to United Arab Emirates, I wrote down the dream I had before my departure from Ghana. I sent a copy to Professor Abadoo in Ghana. I didn't receive any reply until I came back from the sponsored trip.

This was the email I got from the referred professor when I returned to Nigeria:

Dear Segun,

I saw the review of the article and I was thrilled. Why didn't you send initially, the beautiful piece you just sent to me?

I forwarded a copy of what you sent to all the members of the panel and they were amazed at how you used the allegory of the animal kingdom to paint the picture of how the political hegemony, religious aristocracy and economic class form an unholy alliance to improvise and decimate the people of Nigeria and Africa at large.

All of us unanimously agreed that if you had sent this earlier, you would have won the coveted award and become a global ambassador for an affiliate international donor organisation. However, due to the originality of your work, you have been selected as one of the speakers at a pan African conference in Dakar Senegal on the theme: The African Privileged Class and suffering masses. The date and venue will be communicated to you before the end of the month.

Keep it up.

Prof. W. A. C Abadoo

Immediately I finished reading the text, I sighed, then, I murmured to myself: dreams are the best interpreters of our most hidden intentions.

CHAPTER SEVEN

CONCLUSION

We can deny reality, we can challenge it, we can persecute those who point our attention to it - but the fact remains that we can't destroy it.

The reality is that there is a triangle of evil that is made up of the political, religious and economic classes that have formed an unholy alliance to deliberately impoverish, decimate and incapacitate the people so that the members of this evil alliance would continue to control the minds of the people and the wealth of the nation. This is not peculiar to a particular nation, but it is the ontological design that runs the clock of the world.

BOOK TWO

CHAPTER ONE

AT THE PAN-AFRICAN MEETING

I had a great time at the Pan-African meeting where I was invited to give a speech. I challenged my audience to do something about the worsening humanitarian crisis in Northern Nigeria. I argued that fundamentally what was wrong with Nigeria was the lack of structures to address the perennial problems. Furthermore, I spoke about the loopholes that people in power explore to siphon the wealth of the country. I submitted that the weakness of our system made it possible for anyone in power to carry out illegalities and get away with it. One of the Western journalists that came to cover the event asked how strong the judiciary was in my country. I didn't want to give a direct answer. I just said, it was as strong as how the powers that be made it and as weak as they wanted it to be.

Within a month after I returned, I got another invite. This time around, the Students' Union of the University of Ibadan asked me to give a lecture during their annual students' week. I was to speak on the topic: The mistakes of the nation's founding fathers. I did a lot of research on the amalgamation of the Northern and Southern protectorates, the constitutional conferences between 1930 and 1960, the agitation for independence, and so on. While

I was putting my paper together, I wrote a short drama to capture what I thought were the mistakes of the founding fathers which brought us to the abysmal situation that the country finds itself in today.

A week before I went to the University of Ibadan (along with my makeshift drama troupe), I had another dream. The most surprising thing about this dream was that I found myself on the same tree, in the same village, with the same set of animals...

CHAPTER TWO

I HAD ANOTHER DREAM

In my dream, I saw Snake in his office. He looked so agitated. I saw his chief of staff, Lizard, and his personal assistant, Wall Gecko, standing in from of him, obviously very nervous.

After what seemed like about an hour, I saw a long file of Soldier Ants moving furiously to the anthill where they were slated to hold a meeting with Snake. Soldier Ants seemed to me like the representatives of the people or executives of the labour union. They came to present to Snake the problems in their village. The deafening, discordant sounds from Soldier Ants did not permit me to understand what the agitations were all about. The only odd creature I saw among the ants was Parrot. I suspected that he came to report what transpired between Soldier Ants and Snake.

After a while, I saw the leader of Soldier Ants. His head was twice the size of the head of the rest. He leaned on the log of wood in front of Snake and started listing out all the issues that brought them. He listed among others that the portion that Lizard and Wall Gecko appropriated to themselves from the village honey was too much. He said that Snake and his wife did not care whether other animals died or not, what they bothered about was how to remain in power forever. He complained about how Hyenas killed people from North to South. He accused Snake of shielding Hyenas because he, Snake, was the Chairman of the Hyena Association. He complained about the brutality of Tortoise and his cronies. He also complained about the high cost of honey.

Snake listened to all the allegations. Despite being very furious, he remained calm. He stood up and addressed Soldier Ants. He promised to look into all their agitations and find amicable solutions to them. However, he did not allow Parrot to talk.

After a meal of hot mushroom, Soldier Ants moved out of the meeting hall. While on their way, Lizard beckoned on the leaders of Soldier Ants union to return for a private meeting with Snake. By the time they got there, Snake gave them a gallon of honey each. They were very happy. He told them to help keep all Soldier Ants quiet. He also said they should go from North to South to speak well about Snake, Lizard, Wall Gecko, Hyenas and Tortoise. There were only seven big headed Soldier Ants that attended the meeting. While others were matching home under the hot sun, these leaders were sharing the honey. Though all Soldier Ants had earlier planned to carry out nation-wide demonstrations over the inequalities in Airegin village, nothing was heard afterwards. When the representatives of all the animals came for feedback from the leaders of Soldier Ants, the leaders simply told them that they all had to be patient, since Snake needed more time to fix a devastated village which previous leaders had destroyed. Though the representatives of all the animals were disappointed, they all went home with little pints of honey. As they licked the honey on the way, they shook their head in despair, and wondered whether anything good could ever come from the village and the village heads, since every agitation was settled by a share of village honey.

From the position where I sat, I could see a group of Soldier Ants that formed small clusters. I noticed that they neither ate the hot mushroom served at the Ajuba nor took pints of honey shared by leaders of Soldier Ants. They were very small in body size and numerically small. I saw them enter into a small anthill and start planning on how to remove the corrupt heads of Soldier Ants Union so that Airegin village would have a ray of hope. While they talked amongst themselves, I noticed some bigger Soldier Ants surrounded the anthill where the coup d'état was being hatched, poured honey around the anthill and burnt it down. None of the agitating Ants escaped. As I turned around on the tree where I was seated, I saw Lizard carrying a giant sized container of honey to the leaders of Soldier Ants who just carried out the arson against their own group. He congratulated them for being patriotic and gave them a special message from Snake.

I thought that day was specifically separated for protest across Airegin village. I also saw Dragon Flies from the part of the village where the largest quantity of honey was found trouping out in their numbers. They kept shouting, "our oil is sweet, but our soil is bitter." I saw them swamping around in anger but nobody in Airegin village paid attention to them. But after a while when their population had doubled the initial size, I saw Wall Gecko with a small paper in his hand. He was nearly mobbed by the agitating Dragon Flies. But when they saw the fierce looking Hyenas that accompanied him, they backed off. He read the goodwill message from Snake to them. He said Snake understood what they were going through and he would set up a committee that would look into their problems. He said the committee would have access to a large quantity of honey and would have sponsored trips to Mini-Paradise from time to time. Afterwards, he asked Dragon Flies to choose ten of them to be part of the committee.

What I saw next made me very sad! Rather than present the problems that brought them so that Snake's representative would understand the plight of their community, they started fighting amongst themselves over those that would make up the committee. The fight was so fierce that there were several casualties. Since they could not settle on which of them would be part of the Honey Land Development Committee, Wall Gecko gave them several gallons of honey to share amongst themselves and instructed them to send the list to him later.

I also saw Houseflies around Sogal, swarming around in angry protest claiming that Hyenas were killing other animals at will. They wanted to go to Ajuba to meet Snake in order to report the brutality of Hyenas, but they neither had the means to fund the journey nor the numbers to get the attention of Snake and his close associates. So, they called Parrot to help them report the case to everyone that cared to listen. Though Snake heard about the agitations of Houseflies, he did not deem it fit to send any of his close allies to address the protesters. Rather, he instructed the head of Hyenas to ask his killer squad to reduce the number of animals he killed in a week so as not to create chaos or cause unnecessary agitations. He also instructed the head of Hyenas to change some of the leaders known for extreme brutality and post them to different part of Airegin village.

From the middle of Airegin village, I saw Elephant sitting on something that looked like a large fodder of grass. Several animals came to him to settle knotty issues between them and their neighbours. I saw a one-eyed Sheep that had blood stains all over his body. He was terribly in pain. From the distance, I heard him complain about how the representative of Chief Hyena brutalised him because he requested that Sheep should carry him on his back to a village function. Sheep refused such oppression and the result of that refusal led to a bloodied nose, loss of right eye and deep cuts all over the body. Sheep humbly requested for justice to be done in that case. Elephant sighed and signalled that Sheep should see him in private. In what seemed to be an instant, I saw Elephant and Sheep beside the tree I was sitting on. From the vantage position I was able to hear their conversation very clearly.

Elephant: I heard what you said in court and I sympathise with you.

Sheep: Yes, your Lordship.

Elephant: For this case you can never have justice!

Sheep: Why? Is the judiciary no more the hope of the common man?

Elephant: Which judiciary? I am a servant of Squirrel and a slave of Snake. Wherever they push me, there I go!

Sheep: This is unbelievable! So, a common animal cannot have justice in Airegin village!

Elephant: He can! Yes, he can!

Sheep: How, your Lordship?

Elephant: If he can give me some honey. I know how to make Snake and Squirrel compromise in some cases where I have special interest.

Sheep: Why do you have to get some honey for that?

Elephant: I need to bribe Parrot to make noise about that case so that the Town leaders show interest in the case. This will compel Snake to allow justice to be done...

CHAPTER THREE

MY CONCLUSION

The oppressed masses put their trust in those who only give them listening ears; but have already sold their souls to their oppressors.

I woke up with tears in my eyes; and a heavy burden in my heart. Apart from the first triangle of evil, there exists another triangle which is as wicked as the first one. It is the triangle made up of the dependent, compromised and overtly corrupt judiciary, bribe taking labour unions and oppressive law enforcement agents.

BOOK THREE

CHAPTER ONE

THE GRAND CONSPIRACY

My presentation at the University of Ibadan was so controversial. I had a tough time during the question and answer session with one Professor Ibiyemi of the History Department. He was a thorough bred Yoruba man. He was angry at the way I reconstructed the Nigerian history to portray the founding fathers as being passive players in the conspiracy theory to under develop Nigeria. He also frowned at how I held them culpable for being part of the continuous intellectual and economic enslavement of Nigerians through multinational corporations, religious institutions and international organisations. He argued that the pan-African writers had foreseen the evil ahead and wrote extensively about it. He handed me a scholarly article which he just submitted to a foreign journal titled: *Don't blame the past for the present failure.*

I collected the paper from the learned professor, took a few photographs with the students' union leaders and drove to my hotel which was not too far from the campus. Later in the day, one of the students' union leaders visited me in the hotel. She was a beautiful lady of about 21. She spoke English like a native speaker and her set of teeth were as white as pure wool. Her legs were straight and her gown had a foreign label. She carried a foreign handbag. She wore a Brazilian wig.

When I got a call from the reception that one Morenike from the University of Ibadan wanted to see me, I was surprised. I had met her during the programme. She was a beauty with brains. I asked the receptionist to give her my room number and show her the way.

When she entered, I felt very uncomfortable. I really didn't know what she came for. I didn't want to pre-empt her. I asked her to sit on the only chair in the room while I sat on the bed. She was such a delight to be with and to talk with. She told me about herself and her plans for the future. She was the only daughter of the former Ambassador of Nigeria to The Netherlands. Her mother was an American. She asked me to tell her about myself. I was taken aback. I didn't know what to say. After about 30 seconds of thinking very hard, I started by telling her the course I studied at the university. I told her that I was unemployed at the moment, but had plans to establish a school, become a public speaker and a writer. She listened to me quietly and informed me that she had done a lot of background checks about me. She told me that she had read over 50 of my articles. She gave me some information that I thought only my University colleagues knew. She told me that she loved how I string words together to paint an exquisite philosophical ideology or to explain a concept. I told her that my training in the faculty of education made me treat my readers as students. She said she would like us to become friends and that she would like me to meet her dad.

I thought I was dreaming! Of course I didn't understand what being friends was all about. She saw that I was a bit confused. She clarified it by saying that, when she informed her father that I would be coming to UI to give a talk, and her father said he would like to meet me in person so as to know my stance on some knotty national issues and international politics. I was a bit relieved. I thought being friends meant being lovers; and my heart was with someone special.

Before she left, she gave me her number and asked me to call her whenever I was ready to meet her father who was living in Victoria Island, Lagos. I called her at the end of that week and we made an arrangement of how to meet her father.

I knew I was to meet a big-time diplomat and an international business man. I took a cab that drove me to the address I was given. I was ushered in by a security man. I saw Morenike running towards me. I didn't know what to do. It was my first time in Victoria Island. She embraced me and held my hand as if we had been friends for ages. She led me to a private room where her father was waiting for us. There were four chairs in that room. It had a projector and a giant-sized screen. There were many assorted wines on the table.

The man, Chief Olowookere, shook my hand and showed me a seat. He said he had heard a lot about me. He asked me how much it would cost to build my proposed school. I told me it would cost 20 million naira. He smiled and said that would be a substandard school. He said his friend that he contracted to come with an estimate said it would be between 70 to 100 million.

I didn't get his point. But I was silent. He said he would give me a loan of 100 million which I would pay after 10 years with 0% interest rate. I knew for the past few months I had been having strange animal dreams, but the one I just had was the weirdest dream of all. Was this a dream? I looked at Morenike and hot tears ran down my cheeks. I kept on murmuring to myself, "Morenike, who are you?" Her father knew I was too shocked to talk. I lay on the floor for what seemed to be an eternity, as I pronounced all sorts of blessings on the man and his family. He asked me to get up, so that we could get to the business of the day. Chief took an excuse and left Morenike and I alone in the room.

"Morenike, who are you?" That was all I could muster. Morenike looked at me and said, "I am your angel!" I had read how angels appeared to people and helped them, but this was the first time I saw a human angel. She told me that her father was so impressed that she introduced me to him as her friend. She said her father was worried that she didn't have interest in any man. She told me she had vowed to stay with her father, who remained unmarried since the death of his wife, Morenike's mother. Then I asked her what the expectation of her father was. She told me that her father wanted her to marry a Yoruba man who would manage his vast business empire and would love her the way he loved her mother.

Now, I got the point. That was the reason for the background checks and the 100 million loan with 0% interest rate. To be honest, the little time I spent with Morenike had changed me completely. But what would I do with Sade, the lady I had promised heaven and earth. Morenike knew I was worried about something. She asked, "are you worried about Sade?" That question swept me off my feet! "How did you know about Sade?" I asked, with a frown on my face. "I saw all your comments about her on your Facebook page. Ladies have a way of moving on!"

I spent the whole day in Morenike's house. I talked with her father about promoting indigenous companies. We talked about the *expatriate's* quota system, the imbalance in import and export trade balance, the devaluation of naira, the problem with

1999 federal constitution, the issue of federal character, resource control, Boko Haram, Fulani herdsmen, electronic voting, and so on. He showed me a lot of video clips and asked me to read quite a number of research papers. I left the place by 9 pm. I had my breakfast, lunch and dinner with Morenike and her dad. It was like a family reunion.

I knew Sade would call me while I was with Morenike, so I blacklisted her number. Morenike's dad asked the driver to drop me at home. He gave me a sum of one hundred thousand naira. Morenike said she would visit my house when she finished her final semester examination.

I really needed to decide what to do. I was confused and worried. As I got inside my flat, I knew I had a decision to make. Sade and I had been together for 4 years. I got her during the "early rush" for the 100 level female students. I introduced her to all the bad things the bible said she should not do before marriage. She was 17 when I met her and she was a virgin. She was now in third year. "How will I begin the conversation in the first place!" She had never given me any reason to doubt her honesty and integrity. She was my one and only up until Morenike showed up.

It took me a long time to put myself to sleep and when I did, I had another dream.

CHAPTER TWO

MY DREAM

I found myself on that same ancient tree. *I would like to call* the tree, the Oracle tree. From the tree I could decipher the problems of my people.

I saw myself drenched in the rain. Everywhere was flooded. A lot of animals were washed into the ocean, many of the habitations of the animals were destroyed. Only the habitations of the powerful and the mighty were spared, since their habitations were cast in stones and jelled together by thick honey. They are so strong that nothing could break such houses down: neither rain, nor thunderstorm. After the hour-long rainfall, an uneasy calm came upon the village. The losses of lives and properties left the majority of the animals in a state of mourning due to the irreparable loss.

After the destructive rainfall, I saw Squirrel returning from a journey. He carried with him a broad leaf. There were a lot of inscriptions on the leaf. He kept it to his chest. He was running as fast as he could towards the seat of power at Ajuba.

Unlike all other guests, he and other privileged few like him could come to the seat of power whenever they liked. He entered and handed over the leaf to Snake. I saw that Snake was grinning as he read the content of the leaf. After reading through, he pinned it to the wall of his room. From the distance, I could read some of the content of the pasted leaf. The title was: The town's advice on how to take from the poor to give to the rich. Then I saw Value Added Tax, Increase in the price of honey, exchange rate, inflation, devaluation of money and restrictions of loan to the small business owners. There was other information there, but they were mostly statistical data and figures. I didn't pay attention to those. Squirrel took a long time to explain how each of the economic and monetary policies would be implemented in order to keep the poor perpetually poor. As Squirrel left, I saw Parrot fly in. He was given a blank leaf to copy the content of the leaf that Squirrel brought from the town. He was given a gallon of honey and asked to announce the new policies throughout Airegin village. He flew away immediately after he finished copying, and he did not forget to carry his honey along.

No sooner had he left then I saw Elephant. He came in, in his usual imperial majestic strides. He sat beside Snake and informed him that the laws governing Airegin village should be altered. He pointed out the areas that allowed the poor to easily get justice. Snake asked him to meet with his fellow animals in charge of law in Airegin village to help create a lot of bottlenecks in the judicial process. He also asked them to delay passing judgments and to give conflicting judgments. Before Elephant left, he submitted the list of hard-hearted, incorruptible judicial officers that refused to batter their integrities for the sake of honey. Snake collected the leaf that contained the list, gave Elephant 20 gallons of honey and went inside the inner chamber to meet his disciplinary squad. I didn't see what happened in the inner room but I saw a squad of fierce looking Foxes move at a ferocious speed. They looked at the list and went after all the animals on that list; they maimed some of them, killed some of them and spared some that decided to cooperate with Snake and Elephant henceforth.

I was worried about what went on that day in Airegin village. I couldn't alter anything since I was a powerless, passive observer. Then I saw Lion who sat in a special place in Ajuba area of the village. He had a leaf in his hand containing the vacant positions that must be occupied by qualified animals in the village. I saw a lot of animals come in, to submit a leaf that contained information about them and their work experience. Immediately Lion collected a leaf, he would ask which area of the village the animal came from, if it was the area that Snake came from or the area that was in his good book, Lion would drop the leaf on the right side, if not, he would drop the leaf on the left side. When the exercise was complete and all the animals went back to their homes, Lion gave the leaves on his left-hand side to Housefly who traded in small worms, to use the valuable leaves as wrappings. He took the ones on the right to Snake. Snake asked him to sort it out according to political party affiliations of the applicants. Some were dropped for belonging to Scorpion Democratic Party. Then he sorted it out according to religious affiliation. Those that were members of his party but did not belong to religion he favoured were dropped. The leaves were still more than what was required. So, Snake summoned the party leaders to come and pick the leaves they had a special attachment to. After the exercise, there was now a shortfall of about ten spaces. Then Snake used his prerogative to pick ten leaves at random. That completed the process of selection.

CHAPTER THREE

MY INFERENCE

Law is good, tax is good, federal character in appointments is good. But the political class have manipulated all these elementary particles of a functional society to impoverish and incapacitate the people. Justice is for the highest bidder. Multiple taxation is designed to kill business. If any highly qualified individual does not belong to a favoured religious group or political party in power, his certificate is as good as a tissue paper. A university degree is no more ticket for free meal, except it carries the endorsements of the high and mighty. That is another triangle of evil.

CHAPTER FOUR

ANOTHER TROUBLING DREAM

By the time I woke up I woke up, I was sweating profusely. I saw tears trickle down my cheek. It had been a long time since I had shed tears. I felt I was such a strong man. I felt nothing external could weigh me down. But the situation at Airegin village was so saddening. I felt the animals were unfortunate to find themselves in such a despicable place. It seemed the whole machinery was designed to perpetually make them remain at the same socioeconomic status.

I stayed on the bed without sleeping for about 30 minutes. I reflected on the events that happened the night before. It was at that time that it dawned on me that I wasn't actually crying over the precarious situation of Airegin village but over the personal crisis I found myself in. I couldn't think. It seemed my brain had stopped working. I was in a fix, I found myself in a quandary. Here was I, an unemployed graduate who was preparing for my second degree since I was not given an automatic employment despite finishing with a first class because I didn't have anyone backing me. All I had was social media handles that I used to vent my anger on the system that promoted *godfatherism*, and nepotism of the highest order. Anyway, that was not my primary concern at the moment. I didn't know how to handle Sade who was more or less my part-time live-in lover. She breezed out of campus to spend either a day or two with me, or an entire weekend. How would I tell her that the beauty and the fortune that Morenike brought on the table were irresistible?

In the midst of that confusion, I fell asleep again. Then I met myself on the same tree, the Oracle tree. This time, the power brokers; Snake, Scorpion, Lion, Elephant, Squirrel, etc, were not in the picture. I only saw other animals of little consequence in the village. I saw Butterfly, Dragon Fly and Weevil as they were scooping honey illegally from the honey reserve. I saw them as they built underground reservoir to keep the stolen honey. I was surprised that Butterfly, despite her beauty could partake in such illegality. What really surprised me more was that Parrot was standing on top of a nearby tree, licking honey; despite the fact that he saw these economic saboteurs. I presumed that he feared Butterfly, Dragon Fly and Weevil; but he would make a loud noise if Snake did anything wrong. I thought Parrot was being insincere; he looked the other way when the public honey was stolen by common animals, perhaps because he lived among them and feared that his life might not be safe if he blew the lid, so he ignored the crime of the common animals; or he just felt they should have a share of the honey as well, since the ruling class sat on the major chunk of the honey. On the other hand, if he saw any wrongdoing of the privileged class, he would amplify it because he knew that would put him in a position of strength. Sometimes, he would destroy the image of Snake in public so that he, Snake, could pay him to clean up the image.

Another incident that surprised me was happening simultaneously. The incidents happened at Sogal part of Airegin village. I saw Dogs fighting each other. I saw Cat steal the food of another Cat. I saw animals destroying each other. What bothered me was that the animals that did the most evil were the most critical and the most vocal of all the animals. They did complain about the mega evil of the elites, yet, they did evil at their own micro level. I saw Donkey go to Lion to complain about Sheep. In an instant, I saw that Sheep received an order on a leaf that he had been transferred to work in the most restive area of the town. It seemed all the animals were suspicious of each other, especially if they were from different parts of the village or had differences in religion or political ideology. There were a group of animals which were notorious for evil in the animal village. They were led by Jackal. I saw how they crisscrossed the whole village. They extorted other animals and killed those who resisted them. What alarmed me was that each time they came back, they always converged in the house of Tiger to give him returns. Tiger was not part of the ruling class, but he was as rich as Squirrel. He was the one that controls

Animals Oppressors Group (AOG). Snake and Scorpion feared him. Without him, no party could win an election. In an instant, I saw animals filing out to elect leaders in a particular area of the village. I saw the two leading contenders, Buffalo and Horse begging Tiger for his support. Each one of them brought gallons of honey. When they left, Tiger measured the honey and saw that Horse brought more honey than Buffalo. In an instance, I saw that more animals were queuing up behind Buffalo than Horse. While Peacock, the electoral umpire was counting the animals behind Buffalo, the AOG team came with dangerous weapons and injured the animals that lined behind him. I saw the animals running for their dear lives. Many were wounded, while two animals died. Peacock, who had been arrested by some members of the AOG team, was given a result on a banana leaf to announce. They also gave him several gallons of honey. When he tried to protest, they brought out his only son and attempted to kill him. He was afraid and begged them. He collected the result sheet and the gallons of honey and declared Horse the winner. Several animals grumbled, but after a few minutes they resigned to their fate and went about their business. But I saw that Buffalo was so hurt by the defeat. He went to Elephant to seek a legal redress. I was not able to read the content of his petition, but I heard Elephant ask him to wait for him. He sat down fuming. Elephant then went to Snake to seek his opinion. I didn't hear what they discussed, but what I saw was that Elephant asked Buffalo to come back. I saw that Buffalo kept coming, and Elephant kept asking him to come back. He kept coming back until I saw Horse speaking to Parrot to help him campaign for his second term in office.

CHAPTER FIVE

MY RATIOCINATION

I had identified three triangles that were carefully designed to impoverish and oppress the people. It was a machinery of the state and capitalism. But, what of the innate triangle of evil that resides in citizens themselves. People are quick to condemn the religious, the economic and the political class, but they really don't look inwards and see that the leadership of a society is a reflection of the people of that society. Our leaders are what we are. Our system is a reflection of our mindset. The triangle of greed, selfishness and ethnicity may be largely unseen, but is responsible for the conspicuous evil triangles that affect us all.

CHAPTER SIX

TO BE OR NOT TO BE

Morenike called me early in the morning of the following day, she talked with me for one hour. That was the first time I received a call that long. I had never spent more than 5 minutes speaking to anyone at a stretch, I was always mindful of my airtime. But this sweet angel seemed not to care, she was pouring her heart out about her frustration with love, lecturers' harassments and cultists' threats. I sighed and told her that all those were normal experiences that beautiful girls have to face on the campus in Nigeria. She also asked something on qualitative research methodology she needed little clarifications on. When she was done talking she asked me a question which was to define my relationship with Sade. "When are you going to decide between me or her?" I asked her between her and who. She said between her and her rival Sade. I was shocked. She said she had followed me on Instagram and Facebook for a week and she had seen all I said about Sade. She had also read the profile of Sade on LinkedIn and Facebook. I just brushed the issue aside. But she informed me that she would visit me when she finished her final year examination.

It was her long call that made me not able to receive Sade's call. She actually called several times within that call. She told me how worried she was since the other night. She tried to reach me but it was in vain, I didn't pick up her calls nor return her messages on WhatsApp. She asked for my weekend schedule and asked if she could come over. I asked her to come after the fellowship on Sunday. I had planned to go to a prayer mountain on Saturday to pray over this most difficult decision of my life. Dropping Sade would be inhuman, but getting Morenike into my life would open a huge window of unlimited possibilities in life. And more importantly, I just loved what I saw in Morenike. Sade wasn't bad as well; though naive and a bit reserved. But she was a genius. If not because she was spending some of her time with me, she would have had a CGPA of 5.0, but her 4.89 aggregate wasn't bad at that time. Though eventually she finished lower than that but she graduated with a first class.

That Sunday, Sade came as she promised. She brought raw foodstuffs as usual. She made my soup for the week. She also prepared the food for the day. She did the laundry and set the kitchen in order. She also swept the whole flat and watched the toilet. Unlike before that I would stay with her while she did the chores, that day I pretended that I had fever. While I lay on the bed, I kept on ruminating on what the prophet on the prayer mountain told me. The prophet told me that a wise child would not trade a pure honey for some fried bean cakes. He said that Morenike was God sent and I should not miss the opportunity to gain wealth and greatness in life. When I asked him how God would feel if I left Sade, he only quoted a portion of the bible that said "I will have mercy on the person I would have mercy on." He told me that heaven helps those who help themselves. I gave him the sum of N5,000 and I left.

Here was I with a girl who had literally sold her soul and body to me: a girl who would never believe I could think of something like that, not to talk of planned or implemented such. She left later that night, because she wanted to go and study for a test on campus, in company of her friends, and besides, she didn't want to disturb me because I was sick.

For the next three months I started giving excuses to Sade each time she decided to come over. I encouraged her to vie for the best graduating student. I promised that I would be the one to visit her henceforth. She saw that as a great honour, and as bragging right among her friends. I was a popular writer and activist on campus before I graduated. My colleagues nicknamed me double barrel. They said I was both bad and good at the same time.

As I promised, I usually visited her every weekend. We would hang out at a popular Amala Joint and talk for hours. She would place her head on my shoulder and say she missed me a lot. I knew she wanted to come over for a night with me. I didn't want that. From a once a week visit, I reduced it to once a fortnight. She complained, but I told her I had to spend more time conducting trainings and seminars before I come back for my postgraduate studies. She trusted me; she never doubted whatever I said.

One day I came over to visit her during the week. It was a surprise visit. I called her that I was around. She told me she was with a lecturer and would join me when she was done. As a former campus hot guy, I decided to stroll around and see the new constructions going on and some other new developments. As I moved close to the Faculty of Arts, I sighted Sade from afar, a guy was talking to her. I didn't know what they were discussing. The guy gave her a hug and they both parted ways. The guy looked familiar to me. I couldn't recollect how and where I had seen his face. I saw Sade run to take a shuttle. I turned back and walked as fast as I could to our usual meeting point. She did get there before me. While she was calling me on the phone, I shocked her by hugging her from behind. Unlike our usual practice of talking for minutes before eating, I told her to go and order the food because I was hungry. While she was busy ordering the food, I quickly went through her WhatsApp messages. I couldn't read them, but I saw what I was looking for:

the guy that just hugged Sade. His name was Dare and I saw that their last conversation was around 3:45 am. I wanted to read their conversations but I saw that she would catch me in the process. Before that moment, I never read her messages, nor paid attention to her calls. I trusted her completely.

While we were eating, she received a call and was grinning as she talked with the person for about two minutes. When she dropped the call, I asked who the caller was, she told me it was Dare, a theatre art guy who was...I asked her to stop and concentrate on her food. She was shocked. She had never seen me talk with her in that rude manner before. She had never heard me ask about her conversations with anyone. Though, she normally asked me about my own conversations and did read my messages.

We didn't talk much that day. We ate in silence and when we were done, I told her I had to go and sleep in a friend's house because I had an interview for a vacancy at the American Embassy. She looked at me and asked me if there was anything the matter. She asked why I didn't tell her about the interview earlier. I told her it was an impromptu notice, and that was why I came to the campus to notify her. For the first time since we started dating, I saw a look on her face that showed that she was not convinced I was telling the truth. She wanted to give me money, but I turned it down, rather I gave her ten thousand Naira. She asked me what had been happening between us these days. She used to support me a lot since she has a rich uncle working in Microsoft Inc. in America. Every semester he would send her at least three hundred thousand for her upkeep. She spent most of the money taking care of me.

Before I left the school gate, I asked her who Dare was? She laughed out loud. "Is it because of the lousy campus clown that you have been giving me attitude?" She told me she saw me while I was going through her WhatsApp messages, she only pretended not to. She said, "Segun, I trust you despite the fact that you have a lot of female friends!" Instead of talking about Dare, she only informed me that she knew about Morenike. I asked her how she got to know. She didn't reply until we met ten years after in London. By then, she was married to a young American lawyer of African descent while I was married to Morenike.

My friendship with Morenike grew at a faster rate. We chatted for the better part of the day and I called her at least five times in the day and sometimes in the middle of the night. She kept visiting from time to time. But on each occasion, she refused *anybody* contact between us. Sometimes when she came around and it was time to go to church, she would stay at home reading novels or doing some chores. She was not a church girl like Sade. I asked her what was responsible for her decisions, she said, she was her own *judge, and* she set rules for her morality and social engagements. She told me that she went to church whenever she felt the need to listen to sermons and not for any social interaction and religious identity. But she had high moral standards and was very fair in her dealings with people.

As my relationship with Morenike grew, my relationship with Sade took a turn for the worse. I hardly picked up her calls. In order to deny her access to my apartment, I changed the lock of the main door. She came visiting one day and was unable to get in. She called severally, but I refused to pick up her calls. After trying to see me for several weeks, she was fortunate to meet me at home one Sunday morning. She sat down and asked me a vital question, "are we still good?" I shook my head. She knew what I meant. She said nothing after that. She went to the kitchen, prepared the breakfast, served it, went to do the laundry and afterwards left without saying a word to me. I felt *guilty of* all I did to Sade. I knew I had hurt her so deeply. But, I had to make a choice between the good and the better. I felt sacrificing Sade was what I needed to ensure that all my dreams came to pass.

A week after Sade came visiting, I went to her hostel to check on her and offer some explanations. But I was shocked by what I heard. She had left the hostel apartment and relocated to an off-campus apartment. I tried to get where that was, but I couldn't. I checked her several times in the department but I couldn't see her. It was ten years later when we met in London that she told me what happened to her when I left her.

When Morenike finished her course in U.I, she was posted to Akwa Ibom. She later redeployed to Lagos. We got married within that year. It was an elaborate wedding. Immediately after the wedding, we travelled to United Arab Emirates for our honeymoon. The relationship was normal. But, our home was like a courtroom. We argued over everything. Only a superior argument carried the day. She loved me and respected my opinion. When we got back to Nigeria after three months in United Arab Emirate, London and US, the school I built was officially opened for business. Morenike's dad asked me to put people in charge because he had bigger responsibilities for me.

In the course of the year I was inducted as a member of Omo Eko Group. It was a socio-political association of the power brokers in Lagos State. They were the people behind the scene, but who actually decided the direction of public policies and who was to get what in terms of resources and appointments. I took over as the MD of Longlins Holdings, while Morenike's dad retired so as to spend his weekdays on his farm. That was how he wanted to live the rest of his life.

Within a year, I had become a powerful figure in both the business and the political spaces. I had to change my church to the one that was befitting to my status. Morenike was not interested in her father's businesses; she was interested in blogging and showbiz. She became a big hit and had to travel all over the world to cover events. We hardly spent more than a day in the week together. Sometimes, we normally schedule meetings in foreign countries.

I forgot to relay the dream I had before Sade and I parted ways. It was a very short dream. I saw some Grass Cutters moving from the Northern part of the village to the Southern part. I saw other animals complaining about how these dangerous Grass Cutters eat their grasses and licked their honey. They even trample the smaller animals. I saw some of the animals that were affected giving some honeys to Parrot to help them inform Snake about their plights. When Snake got the report, he sent for Elephant to help him draft the laws to address the agitations of other animals over the issue of Grass Cutters. Elephant advised Snake to create special status for Grass Cutters. Other animals were to concede a portion of their land to Grass Cutters. Elephant also drafted a bill that any animal that committed suicide would be punished. His dead body would be burnt and the ashes scattered over the sea. He also wrote a law banning public procession and demonstration. Elephant also wrote a law that banned animals from carrying out religious duties without licence. When Elephant finished drafting the laws, Snake signed it and Parrot was given some honey to inform all the animals about the new laws. I saw animals groan as they looked for drinking water, grasses and worms to eat. Honey also became so scarce. It was such a depressing situation. Yet, they were forbidden to end their own life. The new law took away the right to kill oneself from all animals. I saw many animals that wanted to cross the sea to Town being turned back by fierce looking Jackals. There was dead silence in Airegin village.

...I became the hottest commodity in town. In the days when I was an activist, I used to criticise the allocation of resources, spoke against official corruption, nepotism, bureaucracy and so on. I advocated for change of the federal system, bicameral legislature, and dependence of the judiciary on the executive. I had a column in an online blog that was titled, "Naked". It was very popular. I had a cult following and people that read my articles more or less became my disciples.

Things had changed; I didn't have time for all those petty affairs. It became impossible for me to write or defend any ideology.

What was on my mind was how to get government contracts and place myself in prime position for the senatorial spot. After seven years in politics, I discovered that the former activists like me were the most corrupt of all. I understood that when one was not rich or had not joined politics, he might do all the talking, but when he has his opportunity, he would join the rush for the national cake. It is not possible for me to count all the former activists like me in the national students association that had gone into politics and are no more interested in the struggle. When I was in the university, I was the students' union secretary; my president later became the speaker of the house of assembly in his state. Two years into office, he was arraigned by Economic and Financial Crimes' Commission for embezzling over 600 million Naira; that was even mild compared to bigger frauds and crimes committed by ex-activists.

My primary concern was how to win the ticket for the senatorial seat in my constituency. I was a loyal party member and I belonged to one of the groups that ruled Lagos. My father in law had made way for me. Everything I enjoyed was through his goodwill. My wife, Morenike, had no interest in politics at all. She tried to persuade me to focus on business and activism, but I didn't want any of those petty stuffs. Some of the things I do presently in business like cooking the account books to outwit the tax officials, promoting foreign goods and going treatments abroad were some of the issues I had spoken vehemently against in the past. When my friends took me on whenever we meet at a joint, on some of my previous stance, I usually made it clear to them that "when a person is poor he is always full of ideas, but when he becomes rich, he faces realities of life. These days we roll with the world, then, we used to see the world roll by."

Each year, I spent millions to bribe government officials in order to win the best contracts in each ministry. Ten percent of the proceed from the contracts belong to the leader of Awa L'Aleko Group, ten percent to the imams, herbalists and prophets that supported me spiritually and ten percent was reserved to oil my political machinery.

Exactly ten years after I split with Sade, I had to attend a conference in London. It was a conference that centred on the alternative power source. It was titled: Life after Oil. Jack Ma was one of the speakers at the conference. That would be my twentieth time of being in UK in the past 10 years.

We were lodged in a five-star hotel very close to the venue of the conference. I arrived at London on the eve of the conference. The reason for this was because I needed the help of an immigration lawyer to help me with some documents. I had broken the immigration law at a time. In fact, I had more than one passport. It was one of the few crimes that I committed as I tried to cut corners to get to the big stage. I wanted to seek advice on how to regularise my status and if possible erase my somewhat dirty past. I knew that some of my political opponents may want to dig up my past. I also wanted to meet an image *laundering* firm to help give me a public bath.

The American lawyer, a handsome young man, met me that *evening,* and we discussed all the details. We agreed on a price and I wired the money to his account. When he was about to leave, he said he wanted me to use a different firm for image *laundering*. He gave me a business card which contained the number I should call. His argument was that it is only a black that can clean up a black properly. Also, only someone who understood a terrain could properly navigate through in the dark. Though, he was a Nigerian, but he was raised in the US. He flew with his wife to London from Los Angeles to meet me and another African leader who was indicted of money *laundering* in France.

When the London based image *laundering* company that I had earlier contacted called me, I made an excuse and in the process I forfeited the consultancy fee I paid to them. Based on the recommendation of the lawyer, I contacted the new image *laundering* and I scheduled a meeting with the new firm. A lady answered my call and promised to come by 8:00am the following morning. There was something about the voice that answered the phone that sounded familiar. It struck a chord in my heart. Could it be Sade's voice? The last time I checked she was in US. And besides, she was too *churchy* to be in image *laundering* business!

I took some Chinese food that night and slept off. That night I didn't have any reasonable dream. It was just as if people were running helter skelter in my dreams. There was so much confusion and hopelessness. I woke up around 6 A.M and recited the Lord's Prayer, I got stuck at some point because I couldn't remember the sequence again, so I stopped.

By 7: 50 A.M, I got a call from the reception that a lady from Transparent Africa wanted to see me. I asked the receptionist to show her the way. In two minutes, I heard a knock, and I asked the lady to come in. I was shocked by what I saw. It was Sade. She just grinned and sat on the chair beside the bed.

"Segun, how are you?" I answered, in the affirmative. She asked after Morenike and the children. I told her that Morenike was fine, and she would meet me in the UK when she was done with a fashion show in Ukraine. I told her that our only son was in a school in China as part of a student exchange programme. He would be there for three months.

"I knew you wanted image *laundering*, I would do it for you!" She said as she looked straight into my eyes. Sade had grown from a naive university girl to a very bold public figure. She informed me that she had profiled me for the past 5 years. She had read everything about me in both Nigerian and international news media.

She then asked me about my relationship with Morenike. I knew the answer she wanted. I didn't want to commit myself. She told me that she knew I wasn't happy with Morenike. She said Morenike's desires to succeed on her own terms had been the impediment of our relationship. Then to the issue I had always wanted to know. What exactly happened ten years ago?!

Sade started the narrative in a comical way. She explained how Morenike came to the campus to beg her to leave me for her. She mimicked Morenike by saying, "please, leave Segun for me. It was the first time of falling in love..." Sade said that Morenike became her close friend and started visiting her every two weeks. While I didn't know where Sade relocated to when she left the campus, Morenike knew about it. Sade informed me that she was sick for a long time and had to be taken to the village, so she deferred a semester. She said she believed that my response to the issue informed her line of action. She said that I broke up with her in the most inhuman manner. She said that it was her grandmother that counselled her not to struggle with Morenike for my love. She said that her grandmother said, "if it was meant to be it would be."

I was in tears. I saw the futility of what I had run after. Morenike was always globetrotting. She even didn't want to have our son. She said she wasn't ready. I had to perforate the male protector that I used in order to get her pregnant. She was furious when she knew she was pregnant and threatened to abort the child. I informed her father who called her to order and counselled her against it. She was a good lady, I informed Sade, but, she was married to her career.

Sade said her husband was just like Morenike, he wanted nothing but wealth. She told me that they only saw each other during the weekends. She also said that she took a course in Image *laundering* because she wanted to travel around with her husband once in a while since he was always involved with high profile African leaders who needed to alter the public perception about their image. "Segun, it has been tough without you," she concluded.

We spent the whole day together, just the way we used to do it in the university days. We lay on the bed together and looked at the possibility of "us!" I knew it would be complicated. But, before Sade left my hotel room, she asked me how I was able to cope with the contradictions of my personal life. She pointed my attention to the fact that most of the things I spoke against were the things I now do. She showed me some of the articles I wrote several years ago. As she stepped out, she whispered something to me: Saint Segun, you just slept with someone else's wife!

CHAPTER SEVEN

CONCLUSION

There is no one that is righteous, no, not even ONE.